A TAD TOO SMALL

THE TINIEST TADPOLE IN THE POND

Written and illustrated by Kirk Dodson

ISBN: 9780578778648

For all the tadpoles I have known.
Alexander, Amy, Angelique, Bobby, Elijah,
Emily, Emmett, Evie, Ian, Jack, Jessy, Jimmy,
John, John Mason, JoJo, Jonah, Joshua, Jude,
Little Michael, Maggie, MaKinzee, Piper,
Reagan, Rebekah, Rhea, Sam, Silas,
Waverly, Will.

A special thank you to the Little Lagoon!
You know who you are!

Once upon a time in a little pond, there lived many tiny animals. The smallest of them all were the tadpoles.

1

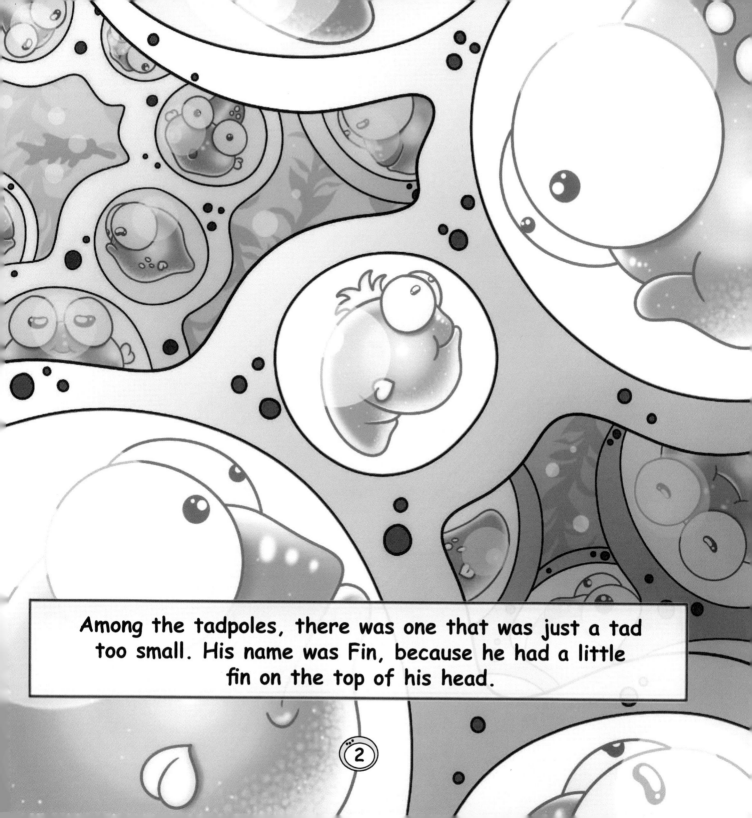

Among the tadpoles, there was one that was just a tad too small. His name was Fin, because he had a little fin on the top of his head.

When it was time for the little tadpoles to hatch from their eggs, Fin was the most excited of them all!

Sadly, Fin was not fast enough to keep up with his bigger brothers and sisters.

Fin loved to watch his brothers and sisters play games like Leap the Lily Pad.

5

Poor little Fin was not big enough to jump over the lily pads!

Fin's brothers and sisters also played a game he did
not like very much. It was called Bounce the Fin.
They would toss poor Fin back and forth
to each other like a ball!

Fin felt sad about being so small. He decided to ask the old snail in the can, "How do I get bigger?" The old snail smiled and said, "You do not have to be big to do big things!"

8

Fin did not like the old snail's answer. Fin decided he would ask someone else how to get bigger.

Fin went to the big green turtle and asked, "How do I get bigger?" The big green turtle said "Sit in the sun. That is what I would do! Surely, it will work for you!"

Fin sat on a lily pad for hours, and all he got was a bad sunburn!

Fin decided he would ask the hungry mudpuppy, "How do I get bigger?" The hungry mudpuppy said, "Eat, eat, eat as much as you can. Surely, that is a great plan!"

Fin ate ate ate as much algae as he could!

"BURP! All Fin got was an upset tummy!

Fin went to the country crawdad next. He asked, "How do I get bigger?" The country crawdad grinned and said, "Hide in a hole till you get big. Come along! I will show you how to dig!"

Fin hid in the crawdad hole for a very long time. He did not get any bigger. He just got lonely.

16

Fin decided he would ask the wandering minnow "How do I get bigger?" The wandering minnow thought for a moment and said, "We will tie fishing line to your head and your tail. We will stretch you out! Surely, it will not fail!"

The fish stretched poor Fin out as far as they could,
but all he got was very sore.

Once again, Fin went to talk to the old snail in the can. "I have tried everything, and I am still small!" The old snail smiled and said, "You do not have to be big to do big things!"

(19)

All of Fin's brothers and sisters had grown into big green frogs, but poor Fin was still so small.

Fin was sad, he just wanted to be left alone.
Then from above something cast a giant scary shadow!

It was a giant catfish! She had come to gobble up the new tadpole eggs! Fin quickly came up with a plan to save them all!

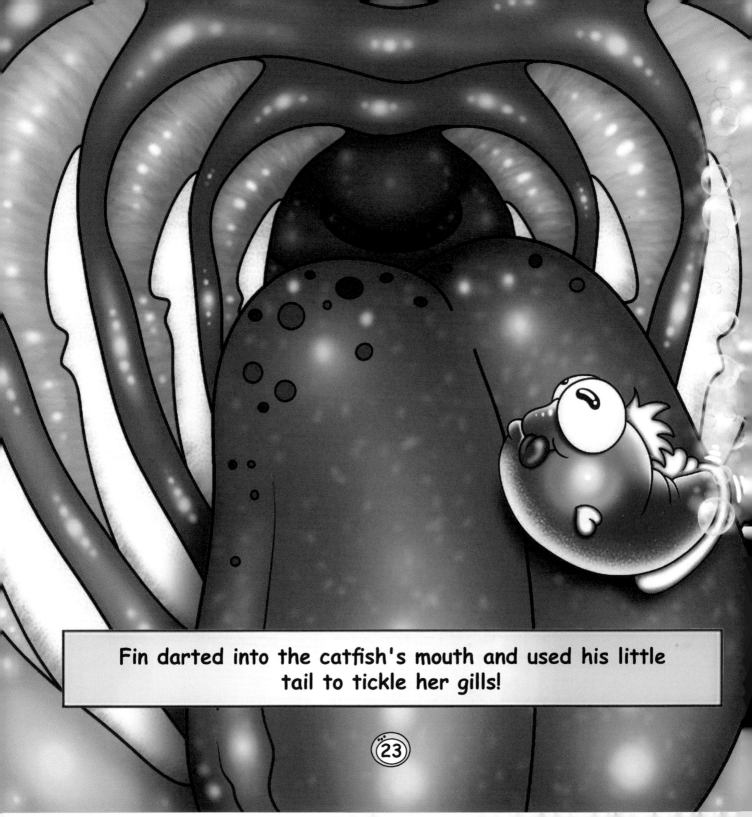

Fin darted into the catfish's mouth and used his little tail to tickle her gills!

23

The catfish started to giggle and gurgle! She cried out, "Little Fin, please exit my gills! I promise, I will never again have tadpole eggs for meals!" Fin quickly shot out of the catfish's gills, as she swam away.

All the little tadpoles in their eggs cheered his name!
Little Fin had saved the day!

The old snail in the can was right after all.
You do not have to be big to do big things!

Kirk Dodson was born thousands of years ago,
On top of a magical mountain in 1976. He spent
his youth singing karaoke with dragons and playing
dodgeball with elves. When Kirk finally went to college,
he earned his bachelor's degree in sculpture
from the Memphis College of Arts. Kirk spent many
years creating art for creatures such as gnomes, goblins,
and politicians. One day Kirk found a wild hair under
a rock and decided to start writing children's books.
It should be noted that Kirk has a GINORMOUS
imagination, and should not be taken seriously!

Printed in Great Britain
by Amazon